D1426537

Aberdeenshire

3108281

HOPSCOTCH
TWISTY TALES

Dick Whittington Gets on His Bike

by Ellen Weeks and David Ouro

W

FRANKLIN WATTS
LONDON•SYDNEY

This story is based on the traditional fairy tale,
Dick Whittington but with a new twist.
You can read the original story in
Hopscotch Fairy Tales. Can you make
up your own twist for the story?

First published in 2013 by
Franklin Watts
338 Euston Road
London
NW1 3BH

Franklin Watts Australia
Level 17/207 Kent Street
Sydney
NSW 2000

Text © Ellen Weeks 2013
Illustrations © David Ouro 2013

The rights of Ellen Weeks to be identified as the author
and David Ouro as the illustrator of this Work have been asserted
in accordance with the Copyright, Designs and Patents Act, 1988.

A CIP catalogue record for this book is available
from the British Library.

ISBN 978 1 4451 1631 0 (hbk)
ISBN 978 1 4451 1637 2 (pbk)

Series Editor: Melanie Palmer
Series Advisor: Catherine Glavina
Series Designer: Peter Scoulding

Printed in China

Franklin Watts is a division of
Hachette Children's Books,
an Hachette UK company
www.hachette.co.uk

For M (Pauline) – EW

Dick Whittington lived in a town
called Little Worth. He had no money
because he could not get a job.

"Can I clean your carpet?"
Dick asked.

"Beat it!" shouted the housewife.

"Can I collect the honey?"
Dick asked.

"Buzz off!" said the beekeeper.

5

"Can I wash your car?"
Dick asked.

"On your bike!" said the man.

"Right," said Dick. "I am off to make my fortune." He jumped on his bike and pedalled out of town.

"Where shall I go? People say the streets of London are paved with gold. I might find a job there," thought Dick.

"Meow!" A black cat followed him.
"Go home, puss," Dick said and
rode off quickly.

Dick huffed and he puffed as he
climbed up the hill.

"Wheeee!" He whooshed down
the other side.

"Meow!" The cat was still following Dick. It looked lonely and lost.

"Let's be friends," said Dick.
"I will call you Lucky." The cat
jumped into the basket and purred
all the way to London.

"Beep! Beep!" There was a huge traffic jam. Dick darted between the cars on his bike.

"Wow! What a busy, exciting city,"
said Dick. "We will find the
gold soon."

There was so much to see –
the London Eye, the Houses of
Parliament, the Tower of London.

The day passed. Still no gold, no job and no money. Dick felt sad as he turned to leave London.

Just then some bells started to ring.

"Turn again, Whittington!"

they seemed to say.

Dick stayed and spent his last coins on a tin of tuna. "This could be our last meal for a while, Lucky."

21

A lady walking past suddenly stopped. "Your cat is exactly what I've been looking for," she said.

"Meet Lucky," Dick said.

"I am Alice," said the lady.

"I want Lucky to be in a cat food advert I am making."

"Lights! Camera! Action!"

Dick really enjoyed watching.

Lucky became a superstar and made Dick a fortune.

"I want to stop traffic jams," said Dick. He spent his money on new bikes and placed them all over the city.

People loved using the new bikes.
Dick became famous. He got the
job of Lord Mayor of London.

Dick and Alice became great friends. Soon they fell in love and decided to get married.

Lucky purred all the way to the church.

Puzzle 1

Put these pictures in the correct order.
Which event do you think is most important?
Now try writing the story in your own words!

Puzzle 2

1. I am looking for my fortune.

2. I look good in front of a camera.

3. I can run very fast.

4. I am looking for a new TV star.

5. I love riding a bike everywhere.

6. I make a lot of TV adverts.

Choose the correct speech bubbles for each character. Can you think of any others? Turn over to find the answers.

Answers

Puzzle 1

The correct order is: 1e, 2c, 3d, 4a, 5f, 6b

Puzzle 2

Dick Whittington: 1, 5

Lucky: 2, 3

Alice: 4, 6

Look out for more Hopscotch Twisty Tales and Fairy Tales:

TWISTY TALES
The Lovely Duckling
ISBN 978 1 4451 1627 3*
ISBN 978 1 4451 1633 4
**Hansel and Gretel
and the Green Witch**
ISBN 978 1 4451 1628 0*
ISBN 978 1 4451 1634 1
The Emperor's New Kit
ISBN 978 1 4451 1629 7*
ISBN 978 1 4451 1635 8
**Rapunzel and the
Prince of Pop**
ISBN 978 1 4451 1630 3*
ISBN 978 1 4451 1636 5
**Dick Whittington
Gets on his Bike**
ISBN 978 1 4451 1631 0*
ISBN 978 1 4451 1637 2
**The Pied Piper and
the Wrong Song**
ISBN 978 1 4451 1632 7*
ISBN 978 1 4451 1638 9
**The Princess and the
Frozen Peas**
ISBN 978 1 4451 0675 5
Snow White Sees the Light
ISBN 978 1 4451 0676 2

**The Elves and the Trendy
Shoes**
ISBN 978 1 4451 0678 6
The Three Frilly Goats Fluff
ISBN 978 1 4451 0677 9
Princess Frog
ISBN 978 1 4451 0679 3
Rumpled Stilton Skin
ISBN 978 1 4451 0680 9
Jack and the Bean Pie
ISBN 978 1 4451 0182 8
**Brownilocks and the Three
Bowls of Cornflakes**
ISBN 978 1 4451 0183 5
Cinderella's Big Foot
ISBN 978 1 4451 0184 2
Little Bad Riding Hood
ISBN 978 1 4451 0185 9
**Sleeping Beauty –
100 Years Later**
ISBN 978 1 4451 0186 6

FAIRY TALES
The Three Little Pigs
ISBN 978 0 7496 7905 7
Little Red Riding Hood
ISBN 978 0 7496 7907 1
Goldilocks and the Three Bears
ISBN 978 0 7496 7903 3
Hansel and Gretel
ISBN 978 0 7496 7904 0

Rapunzel
ISBN 978 0 7496 7906 4
Rumpelstiltskin
ISBN 978 0 7496 7908 8
The Elves and the Shoemaker
ISBN 978 0 7496 8543 0
The Ugly Duckling
ISBN 978 0 7496 8544 7
Sleeping Beauty
ISBN 978 0 7496 8545 4
The Frog Prince
ISBN 978 0 7496 8546 1
**The Princess and
the Pea**
ISBN 978 0 7496 8547 8
Dick Whittington
ISBN 978 0 7496 8548 5
Cinderella
ISBN 978 0 7496 7417 5
Snow White
ISBN 978 0 7496 7418 2
**The Pied Piper
of Hamelin**
ISBN 978 0 7496 7419 9
Jack and the Beanstalk
ISBN 978 0 7496 7422 9
The Three Billy Goats Gruff
ISBN 978 0 7496 7420 5
The Emperor's New Clothes
ISBN 978 0 7496 7421 2